W9-ACX-226

Dinah's Mad, Bad Wishes

For Nancy and Ann,
sisters and friends.

Library of Congress Cataloging-in-Publication Data
Joosse, Barbara M.
  Dinah's mad, bad wishes / by Barbara M. Joosse ; pictures by
Emily Arnold McCully. — 1st ed.
      p.   cm.
  Summary: Dinah wishes horrible things for her mother when
the two have a fight.
  ISBN 0-06-023098-3 : $ ISBN 0-06-023099-1 (lib. bdg.) :
$
  [1. Anger—Fiction. 2. Mothers and daughters—Fiction.]
I. McCully, Emily Arnold, ill. II. Title.
PZ7.J7435Di   1989
[E]—dc19   88-884
                                                     CIP
                                                     AC

Dinah's Mad, Bad Wishes

by Barbara M. Joosse

pictures by
Emily Arnold McCully

Harper & Row, Publishers

"Dinah Louise, I'm very, very angry with you!"

"Well, I'm mad at you, too!"

"That will be enough, young lady!
Go to your room!"
"O-KAY!"
"Okay!"

7

Dinah slammed her bedroom door.
Ka-BLAM! The noise felt good.

Dinah pushed a chair against the door so
Mama couldn't come in. Then she piled her
books and her stuffed animals on top.

That Mama! thought Dinah. She is mean!

Thwack! Mama slapped the wet washrag against the wall. She scrubbed against the colored marks. The colors spread into the white wall until everything looked gray. *Thwack! Thwack!* The scrubbing felt good.

That Dinah! thought Mama. What has gotten into her?

Dinah plopped into her rocking chair. She rocked back and forth, back and forth—hard. *Bump bump.* The rocking chair bumped against the wall. Dinah wasn't supposed to bump things with her rocker, but she didn't care. Rocking made Dinah feel good.

Bump bump. Mamas are supposed to be nice and not yell, thought Dinah.

Mama scrubbed so hard the paint came off the wall.

I just painted that wall and now it looks terrible, thought Mama. She threw the washrag into the bucket. Water splashed all over the floor, but Mama didn't care.

11

Mama got on her Exercycle. She pushed
hard at the pedals to make the wheels go fast.
Whizz. Whizz. Pedaling made Mama feel good.

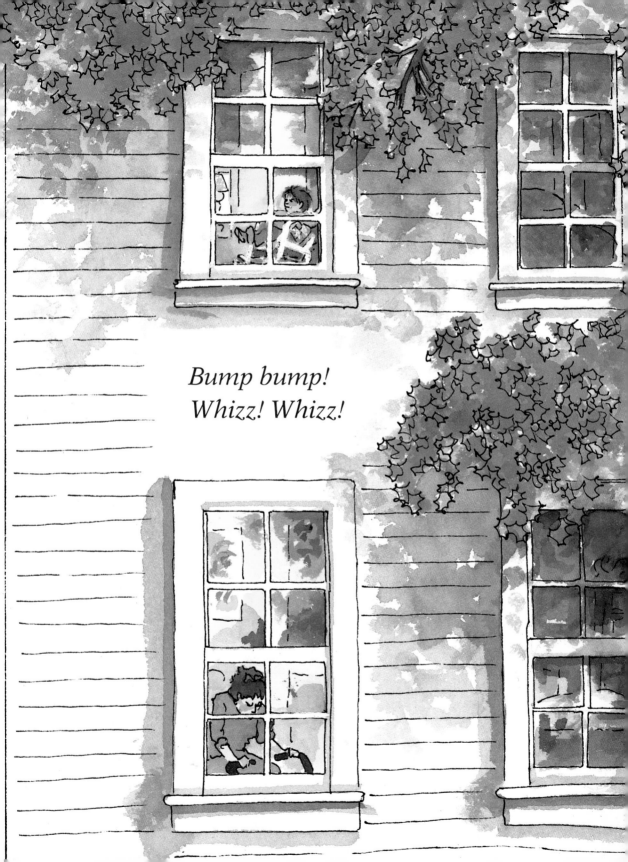

Bump bump!
Whizz! Whizz!

Bump bump! I'm so mad at Mama I wish her ears would fall off her head and warts would grow all over her face, thought Dinah. I wish her nose would turn into a fat sausage and her hair into spaghetti. And then she would look in a mirror and see how ugly she looked and the mirror would crack. *Then* she would cry about it and be sorry for yelling at me.

Whizz! Whizz! Mama pushed the pedals harder. The spinning wheel flashed silvery and bright in the sunlight. Mama was sweating and her face was red.

I wish I'd never bought those colored markers for Dinah, Mama thought.

Bump bump! I wish a vampire would come
after Mama. Mama would try to get away,
but the vampire would run after her. Then
the vampire would bite her neck, but he
would spit out the bite. "You taste too mean,"
he would say.

Whizzzz. Mama wiped the sweat off her
face with her sleeve. When I was Dinah's age
I cut a magic cape out of my mother's
curtains. Boy, was she angry!

18

Bump bump! I wish a witch would tie Mama
to a broom and fly off into the night sky.

The witch would have bloody eyes, and when she looked at Mama, Mama would be scared and cry.

"I told you to be nice to Dinah," the witch would say.

"Please take me home. I have to take care
of Dinah!" Mama would beg, but the witch
wouldn't listen.

Mama would have to be on the witch
broom forever. *Then* she would be sorry for
yelling at me. She would be scared, too, and
lonely.

She would really miss me then.

Dinah stopped bumping and rocking. She felt hot outside and cold inside.

What if my wishes come true? she thought. What if a witch takes Mama into the night sky and keeps her tied to a broom and Mama never ever comes back?

"I'll save you, Mama!" cried Dinah through the door.

Quickly she pulled away the stuffed animals and the books. She pulled away the chair and flung the door open.

And there was Mama!

Mama's face was smooth. There were no ugly warts or a sausage nose. Mama didn't look angry anymore.

She was smiling.

"Dinah!" cried Mama, opening her arms
wide for a hug.

"Mama!" cried Dinah, running into the hug.

31

Mama and Dinah hugged for a long, long time. They had whizzed and bumped and wished their angry feelings away.

Now only the loving was left.